Little Fish

by Ralph Moisa Jr.

Perfection Learning®

Cover and Inside Illustrations: Dea Marks

About the Author

Ralph Moisa Jr., a descendant of the Yaqui Nation, has spent many years researching the history and customs of many American Indian tribes, including his own. For over 20 years, he has performed and presented Indian history across the United States. He strives to help all people see the Indian world through an Indian's eyes.

Mr. Moisa also serves the Indian community and speaks in support of Indian causes. Using his own experiences, he warns against the dangers of prejudice and emphasizes the numerous benefits of a diverse society. In this way, he hopes to help people understand and appreciate all races.

Mr. Moisa currently resides in Des Moines, Iowa, with his wife and two children.

Dedication

This story is dedicated to my son Bryan. He has not yet discovered that he, like Old One, is a teacher. His first student was me. He taught me how to be a father and a dad. I did not learn all the lessons smoothly or well, but I tried. I hope that when he recalls the words of this story, he will accept the responsibilities of a teacher. That he will start with his sister and guide all the "Little Fish" he meets down the right path. The path that will save them from destruction. That will save them for the future. I love you, son.

Contents

Introduction

I want to tell you a story about Little Fish. First I must explain. Fish People are not the same as Two-Leggeds.

The Fish People live in water. Not on land as we do.

Our young are born one or two at a time. It is not the same with the Fish People. Many of them are born at once.

It's true we're not the same as the Fish People. But we are no more important.

We depend on them. And they depend on us. We would miss them if they were not here.

The Creator has made a wonderful world.

Now I will start this story.

8

Chapter 1

When Little Fish was born, she was the smallest. All her brothers and sisters were bigger. And that is why she was called Little Fish.

She swam in the river where she was born. Her brothers and sisters swam there too.

It was a small river. But it was the whole world to them.

The Rock People were a part of the river too. They lived where the water was shallow and the shore was sandy. They shared their home with the Fish People.

On the river's edge, there were many Tree People. They spread their branches over the river. They sent their roots into the water.

A little ways downstream, the river
ended. That was where the falling waters
were.

Little Fish would watch as a leaf or
twig went over the edge of the falling
waters. "Where do they go?" she
wondered.

Chapter 2

Little Fish and her family were happy in the river. She and her brothers and sisters grew.

Little Fish was still the smallest. But she knew she was growing. She couldn't fit under her favorite rock anymore.

Little Fish's world was changing too. The falling waters were not as strong. Were the rocks taking up more room? Or was the water level going down? She couldn't tell.

One day as Little Fish was swimming alone, she heard a loud splash. The sound came from the deepest part of the river.

Little Fish swam toward the sound. All the other Fish People swam toward the sound too.

There, in the deepest part of the river, was the biggest fish among them. He was old. And as long as ten of them.

"I am called Old One," he said. "I have come to help you."

Chapter 3

Little Fish was puzzled. "Why do we need help?" she wondered.

Old One spoke. "The seasons are changing. Soon it will become very cold. So cold that the waters will stop flowing.

"The water will become as hard as a Rock Person. Then it will be too late."

Little Fish looked at her brothers and sisters. What did Old One mean?

Old One went on. "Each of you must follow me. We will go to the other side of the falling waters. There you will be safe.

"But it will take a lot of work. First you must swim fast. Then you must jump high.

"You will land in the big water. Where the waters are too deep to freeze.

"We will live in the big water. The plants that lie at the bottom will be our food."

The young ones were full of
questions.

"What is the big water?"

"Why do we have to leave?"

"How can water turn hard?"

"Why should we believe you?"

Chapter 4

Old One just waited and listened. When the talking stopped, Old One spoke.

"There is so little time. I can only answer some of your questions.

"This river is only a small part of the world," Old One began. "The big water is bigger. But it is only a part too.

"I have told you that the seasons are changing. This is something you have not seen before. But I have seen the seasons change many times.

"The waters change from warm to cool to cold. When the water is very cold, it hardens.

"The water near the shore hardens first. But soon it spreads. Until the waters are all one solid rock. That is when it will be too late.

"I am one of your grandfathers. Your families before you have followed me. They live on the other side of the falling waters.

"They are waiting to help you. Just as their families helped them."

Then Old One paused. Everyone waited for him to speak again.

"It is always the same. Some of you will follow me without question. Some will try but will not make it. Some will not even try until it is too late.

"Once the waters harden, it will be too late. Watch me," Old One said. "I will show you how to jump."

Old One swam to the far end of the river. He swam fast. Straight to a large Rock Person. The young ones watched.

Suddenly, Old One jumped out of the water. He sailed over the Rock Person. Splash! He landed on the other side.

How excited the young fish became! They had never seen anything like this before.

"We can do that!" they cried. All over
the river, the young fish swam, jumped,
and splashed. It was a fun game.

Little Fish wanted to jump too. So she
swam as fast as she could. Up she
jumped.

Ouch! Her nose hit the rock. She fell down the smooth side. She had not gone fast enough.

But Little Fish didn't give up. She tried again. This time with a smaller rock.

Splash! Little Fish landed on the other side.

What fun! Little Fish jumped again and again.

Splash! Splash! It felt good to jump out of the water.

Chapter 5

As the fish jumped and swam in the river, Old One just watched. He was pleased to see them jumping.

Then he spoke again. "It is almost time to follow me to the deepest part of the river. There we will jump over the falling waters.

"The jump we must make is a long one. It won't be easy. But if you try hard, you will all make it."

Little Fish was scared. How would she ever jump that far? She wondered if she should try at all. It was so hard being the smallest.

Old One knew what Little Fish was thinking. He spoke to her.

"Little Fish, do not worry. If you try, you will be able to follow me."

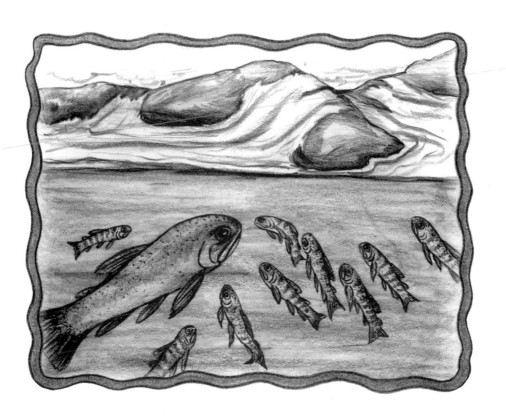

After Old One spoke, he moved on to the others. He spoke to each of them. He seemed to know their thoughts also.

"Now it is time to try the great leap," Old One said.

All the fish gathered at the leaping spot. Little Fish and her brothers and sisters were there.

Some came to try. Some came to watch.

Old One spoke. "Follow me."

He swam fast and hard. Many of the young ones followed him. He rose out and over the falling waters. He disappeared on the other side.

Most of the young ones made it. Little Fish did not.

Chapter 6

Little Fish listened to the others who had not made the leap.

"This is too hard."

"I hurt my nose."

"Maybe we should stay."

"I think I'll try again."

"Try again?" Little Fish thought. Of course! That was it! Old One hadn't said they had to make it the first time.

Little Fish knew what she had to do. She started swimming fast and hard. Back and forth she swam. Over and over she jumped.

This went on for several days. Little Fish didn't know it, but each day she was getting stronger. She swam a little faster. And jumped a little higher.

And then Old One returned. "It is time, my young ones," he said.

Little Fish was scared. "No, I need more time," she said.

"There is no more time," Old One said. "Look at the shores."

The shores were as hard as a Rock Person. A wall of ice stood between Little Fish and some of her brothers and sisters. They were stuck on the other side. It was too late for them.

Little Fish hadn't noticed. She had been too busy jumping in the deepest part of the river.

Old One spoke again. "This is what I told you. It has happened every cold season. Now follow me."

Old One swam fast. The young fish in the deepest part of the river followed.

Up, up, and over the falling waters they went. But not Little Fish. She had just missed.

Little Fish was all alone in the deepest part of the river. She felt sorry for herself. She had worked hard. Why couldn't she make it? Why was she left behind? She had done everything she was told to do.

"I guess I'm just too small," Little Fish said.

Then she thought of Old One's words. "If you try, you will be able to follow me."

"Old One said I could do it," Little Fish thought. "He didn't say I was too small." She knew what she had to do.

Little Fish gathered all her strength. She swam faster and harder than ever before.

She tried again and again. And each time she tried, she grew stronger.

Her fins moved her with such speed. She knew she could do it. She just had to get a good long start.

Chapter 7

Little Fish went to the starting spot. But the water there was frozen. She didn't have room for a long start. What could she do?

She paused to think. Little Fish had worked hard. And she wasn't going to give up now.

Then it came to her. She couldn't go back very far. But she could go down.

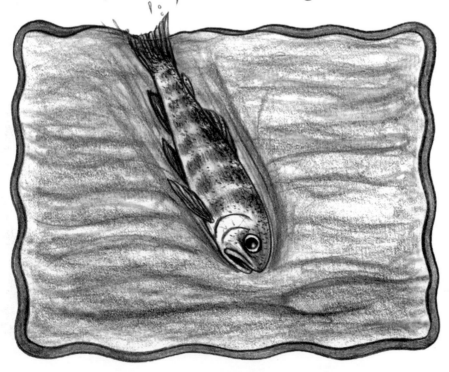

Little Fish knew this would be her last try. She backed up as far as she could. She dove down to the river bottom. Then she raced toward the surface.

She pushed herself upward, using all the strength in her little body. Above the water she flew. The falling waters were coming closer.

And then Little Fish saw something she had never seen before. The big water. It was so big and beautiful. She just had to make it.

Her body was on the way down. Had she jumped far enough?

Splash!

Her strength was gone. She had done her best. And it was just enough. Little Fish had made it to the big water.

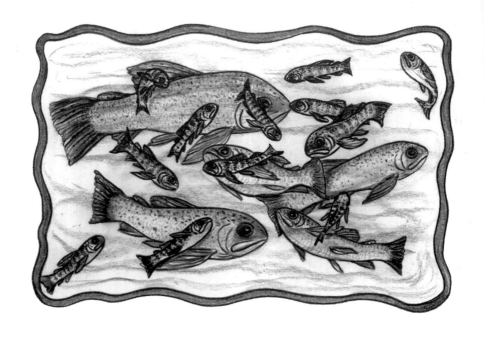

A cheer rang out. "Hooray for Little Fish!"

Little Fish saw her brothers and sisters. Behind them were older fish she had never seen before. They were all happy to have another one join them.

That's when Little Fish heard a familiar voice. She turned and saw Old One.

"I knew you would make it," Old One said. "You see, Little Fish, someone before you had your name.

"It was long ago, before your mother's mother or your father's father was born. There was a young fish. And he was smaller than any of his brothers and sisters. They called him Little Fish.

"But when he grew older and had jumped into the big water, they gave him a new name. They called me 'Old One.'

"Someday you will have my name. It will be your job to bring the young ones to the big water."

The Final Word

So remember, my young friends.
Never give up. And you, too, will see the
big water.

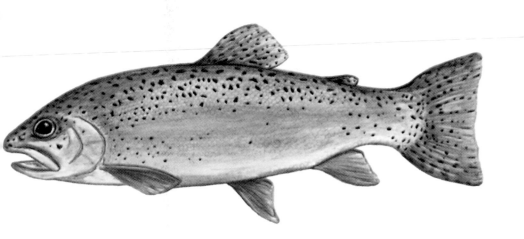

Chapter 8

Little Fish was a rainbow trout. Trout are just one of many kinds of fish.

Trout live and breathe in the water. They sleep on the bottom of rivers and lakes. People breathe with their lungs. Trout breathe through gills.

Trout also have scales and fins. The scales protect their skin. The fins help them swim.

Trout have eyes on each side of their heads. But they have no eyelids. Their eyes stay open even when they sleep.

Some trout live in fresh water. They like rivers and lakes. Some trout live in salt water. They like the ocean.

Some trout like both—fresh water and salt water. They live in rivers in the summer. They move to the ocean in the winter.

Corbis

Trout lay eggs just like birds do. They go to special places called spawning grounds to lay their eggs. Some trout build nests for their eggs. They dig holes in the sand.

A female trout lays many eggs. Then she covers them with loose sand.

But a mother trout never sees her babies. She swims away before they hatch.

Baby trout are very small. They can swim as soon as they are born.

Trout spend their days swimming and eating. They eat plants. They also eat small fish and other small animals.

Some animals like to eat trout. Eagles, owls, and hawks catch trout. They fly over the water looking for their dinner. Then they dive into the water and catch the trout in their strong claws. Bears like trout too. They wade into streams and catch the fish with their

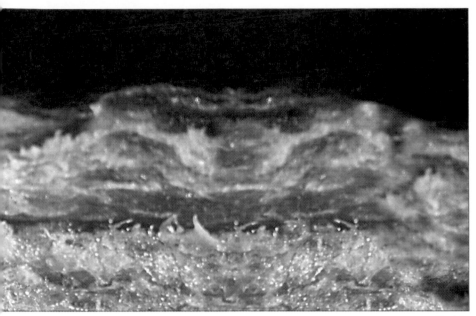

paws. A trout must swim very fast to escape a bear!

Trout must have clean water to live in. Some rivers and lakes are polluted. That means they have poisons in the water. When the water is poisoned, trout die.

We have laws now to protect trout and other fish. It is important for them to have clean places to eat, swim, and lay their eggs.

Chapter 9

Rainbow trout are one kind of trout. They live in rivers and lakes. In the winter, some swim to the sea.

Rainbow trout are beautiful. Their scales are pink, green, yellow, and white. They shine in the sun. Their scales also have little black dots on them. The dots look like freckles!

When rainbow trout move to the ocean, they change color. Their scales become blue and gray. Then they are called steelheads. When they go back to the river, they get their rainbow colors back again.

Look for these other
Cover-to-Cover chapter books!

The Elephant's Ancestors

Great Eagle and Small One

James Meets the Prairie

The Jesse Owens Story

Magic Tricks and More

What If You'd Been at Jamestown?

What's New with Mr. Pizooti?

The Whooping Crane

Yankee Doodle and the Secret Society

56